AF415095

TYPEWRITER REPAIR SHOP

A RIDGE FALLS STORY

TROY LAMBERT

Typewriter Repair Shop
A Ridge Falls Story
Troy Lambert

Published by Unbound Media
© Copyright 2015 Troy Lambert
Second edition 2020.

CONTENTS

PART ONE: THE BEGINNING

It's funny how you get used to some things. Strange happenings.

Hauntings, if you want to use that word.

I was tired of living in a town where they were almost expected. There wasn't a damn thing anyone in Ridge Falls could do to stop them, at least so it seemed.

So, I bought a house in Garibaldi, a small coastal town in another state. I called it a writer's retreat, a place I'd visit occasionally, but even in the beginning I knew it was more than that. The bay reminded me of the reservoir back home, where the water was both dammed and damned. Held back by a man-made structure, and doomed by the supernatural. Yet, Garibaldi Bay was neither of those things. Their only shared trait was a rolling mist.

But the mists of Garibaldi seemed so innocent in comparison. Eventually, I spent less and less time at "home" and more time at the "retreat."

I remember the day a new storefront appeared in what had been a vacant building downtown because it was also the day I put my home in Ridge Falls on the market. The day I realized Garibaldi was home.

New businesses were uncommon in town, even when they made sense. The rocky piece of Oregon shoreline made tourists bypass this little spot in favor of the white sand beaches of Rockaway or the amusement park atmosphere in Seaside. Only two motels stayed open year round, and were rarely full except for during the annual festival. Other than bars and restaurants, most businesses catered to the commercial fishermen or those employed at the Coast Guard base.

Filling my Jeep at the local gas station, I noticed the "For Rent" sign missing from the dusty window front across the street, and was immediately curious.

"Fill 'er up, Mr. Randall?" the attendant asked. I was adjusting to the Oregon law that required the attendant pump the gas, not the customer.

"You bet, Sam," I said over my shoulder, taking a step toward the street.

"You checkin' out the new shop?" he called after me.

"Thought I might."

"Don't bother. Whoever rented it has a heavy blanket over the front window. Can't see in."

"Any idea who it is?"

"Nope. No one seems to."

"Doesn't Ned's family own the place?"

"Yep. But the guy just told him he needed a store space. Paid a year in advance." Sam spat on the ground, as if disgusted anyone would even try to keep secrets in such a small town.

I shared his disgust that secrecy could be so easily purchased.

In Ridge Falls, secrets ruled.

The pump clicked, and Sam handed me back my credit card. "Thanks," I told him, shaking his hand.

The Jeep started on the first crank, and I made a quick U-turn and headed for home.

* * *

With modern computers, it's a rare thing to find a typewriter, but I have one. Once in a while, when I want to write slowly and take my mind back to the old days, when I was a teen and first started writing stories, I type, the keys striking real paper.

I have an old Royal, steel gray, like the one my grandfather gave me as a boy. This one has the same green keys, though the letters are still clear, not worn away like the one I had when I was younger. I found some ribbons and stockpiled a lifetime supply. A friend told me I could re-ink them myself, but the last thing I needed was another hobby requiring another set of specialized equipment.

Somehow the idea of a new shop in town inspired me. Back at my cottage, I went straight to the desk the Royal called home and sat in the old fashioned chair I'd purchased to match the machine. I rolled a sheet of paper into the carriage, and put my fingers on "home row."

There are times when I sit down, ready to write, with no idea what words might begin the story. It's like an itch in the mind. Words are the only cure, a calamine lotion for the desire to create. This was one of those times.

The keys clacked, a sound both familiar and foreign.

She never would have built the house there, if only she had known.

Who was she? I would have to keep typing to find out.

The house overlooked the bay, and the address on her mail

said Bay City, but she claimed Garibaldi as her home no matter where the truck came from that delivered her letters.

Usually in tune with the world around her, the truth of this house kept itself hidden from Ethel until it was too late.

Little dark, don't you think? I told myself after reading the first few lines.

My fingers found the keys again.

Ethel had drawn her own plans, then delivered them to a local architect. He frowned, but when she insisted, he simply re-drew them to scale, and two days later she picked up the draw-ings and took them to the building department, such as it was.

Nobody did much construction in Garibaldi, at least not where she had chosen. Usually the only way it was geographi-cally possible was if an older structure on the lot was torn down. Or burned. Even more rarely, a home slid into the bay due to a sub-standard foundation or shifting earth.

The building inspector, who also played many other roles, shook his head and looked puzzled as well, but didn't say a word.

Some stories come to you, whispered like secrets in your ear by many voices. This one came to me shouted, Ethel insisting I tell her story.

I rolled in another page. Kept typing. Considered switching to the computer, but the story seemed to be flowing this way.

Sometimes as a writer, you don't fuck with a flowing story. If it's coming, you just let it come. Ethel's story was a brewing hurricane.

It took them only four months to build the house. At least the outside. Ethel started to fill the inside, finding herself pickier than usual. This room had to have this flooring, this furniture, arranged just so. Her taste was declared impeccable by the merchants, most from out of town. Where would she find such quality pieces locally?

No one questioned her choices. Why would they? There was no way they could have known. She didn't know herself.

It wasn't until her neighbor came to visit that she realized something was terribly wrong.

"Hi, Ethel. How is the decorating going?"

The driveway to the house was a shared one, and the two neighbors had met early on. Naomi did not seem to mind the constant deliveries, though she occasionally scowled at the large trucks as they dropped off Ethel's purchases and negotiated the tight turnaround.

"It's going well," she told her neighbor. "Would you like to see?"

"Sure," Naomi said.

She rushed past Ethel, almost pushing her out of the way. The older woman smiled, preening as she pointed out living room favorites, explaining the origin of each piece in a loud voice. At least, what she believed to be their origin.

The living room tour went well, at least she thought so.

But Naomi looked pale. She wasn't as talkative all of a sudden.

"Do you not feel well?" she asked. "We can do this another time."

"No, I'll be fine," the woman told her.

"Let's go to the kitchen. I'll get you some water, or perhaps a glass of wine? Going on about myself, I have been a horrible hostess."

"S-sure," Naomi stammered, and followed.

As they crossed the threshold, Naomi pointed at the dining room table and screamed.

Not a 'there's a mouse' scream. A scream of pure terror.

"Naomi, dear?" Ethel asked.

But the woman's hands covered her mouth, her eyes wide.

Like she was seeing a ghost.

"Dear?" Ethel asked again, reaching out a hand.

As I finished that line, I found I was sweating, although it was not hot in the front room. In fact, far from it. It seemed colder than normal.

I hit the return lever, and the paper slid out at an angle. There were times when I first started writing that I typed right off the end of the page and had to retype a few lines. For the first time in years, I had almost done it again.

My stomach growled, and I headed for the kitchen. The fridge was empty, and I decided I needed to get out of the house and find a burger and a beer. Maybe some groceries even.

I grabbed my jacket and keys, but before I could make it to the door, I felt a sudden pull.

I couldn't leave yet. The story was calling me back.

Before I realized it, I was sitting in front of the Royal, rolling in another sheet of paper.

* * *

Ethel continued to get deliveries. She filled the house rapidly, until one day she decided she was done.

She had no idea why she felt at that moment the house was complete, but there was no doubt in her mind.

Everything just looked . . .

Right.

There was no other way to put it.

Two days passed. Three. Ethel worked around the garden and the yard, for although she had a service to do most of the gardening for her, she liked to get her hands dirty.

Trim a rose bush here or there. Water the rhododendrons. It seemed reasonable that while she walked, she could also be working.

On the third day Naomi came over. She tentatively knocked.

Ethel of course, let her in. Offered her coffee, as it was before eleven, and any beverage other than water would be impolite to share, especially in social company.

Naomi walked in. Everywhere she looked she stared.

"Ethel, where did you get the ideas for this décor?" she asked.

"The ideas just came to me. The pieces just seemed to fit."

"That makes no sense," her neighbor said. "Do you know what happened here before you moved in?"

"The realtor spoke of a crime, but I told her I wasn't concerned."

Naomi stared.

"Should I be?" Ethel aske un er her gaze.

Damn it. The 'd' on the old machine was suddenly malfunctioning. Just what I needed. No matter.

I'd switch to the computer.

I rolled out the last page and took it over to my other desk.

Interrupted the screen saver, which spun 3-D text: WRITE ON.

Clever.

Opened my favorite word processor.

Looked at the last line.

Typed in:

"Should I be?" Ethel asked under her gaze.

And stared at the cursor. The story that had been flowing so freely was at a standstill.

I had no idea what Naomi would reply. What Ethel would say next.

Nothing.

Shit.

I'll just write it longhand, I told myself.

Opening the cabinet drawer, I dug out a yellow notepad I kept for this purpose.

Sat down and hand wrote the sentence:

"Should I be?" Ethel asked under her gaze.

And nothing.

No idea what would come next. I was stuck.

Walked back to the typewriter, and rolled the sheet back in.

"You shoul ," Naomi sai . "Because you've re ecorated the place back to exactly how it was when the mur er happene ."

"The mur er?" Ethel aske .

I stared at the keys. The 'd' was there. But clearly not working. Now what? Turning the typewriter toward me, I looked at the rack of metal strikers. Pressed the 'd' slowly and studied the striker arm as it rose. There did not appear to be anything wrong with it.

Until it struck the ribbon, and the paper, and had no effect.

I decided to take a break. Go into town and think about the story. Maybe grab some fish and chips out on the pier.

As I drove past the gas station, I saw the new store. I noticed because through the Garibaldi gloom, the lights brightened the sidewalk.

The window was no longer covered.

A sign in the window declared the shop open.

And over the door, a sign stated the name and nature of the business.

"Typewriter Repair Shop," it read.

I swerved to the curb and stopped.

Looked in the window to see a row of Smith Coronas, Underwoods, and Royals, typewriters very similar to my own.

Without thinking, I went inside.

PART TWO: FIXED UP

A bell rang over the door as I entered. A man leaned over an old Remington, a jeweler's loop at his right eye, a small pick or screwdriver in his right hand.

He wore white gloves with ink-stained fingertips.

The store smelled like an old print shop. Aging paper, ribbons, rubber, and dust mingled to form one of the most pleasant scents I'd ever encountered. I wasn't a candle guy, but if I could have somehow bottled this smell, put it in wax and lit it in my writing room, I felt I would never lack for inspiration.

As I looked around, Ethel's story swam into my mind, not because I knew what happened next.

Because I needed to know. I needed to get back.

The proprietor looked up at me, one eye unnaturally large in the loop. He took it off, and it dropped to his chest on a cord. He smiled, one of those "You're interrupting me, but I have to be nice to you" customer service smiles you get from time to time.

"Can I help you?"

"Can you repair an old Royal?" I asked, immediately feeling like an idiot.

"Of course," he said. "What seems to be the problem?"

"The 'd' stopped working."

"Stopped working?" he asked. He put down the instrument in his hand and removed the gloves.

"Yes," I said, suddenly nervous as he walked toward me. "I looked at it, but can't see anything wrong with the striker."

"The ribbon is good?" he asked.

"Seems to be," I said. "All of the other letters work."

"But is it good for the 'd' I wonder?" he muttered under his breath.

"What?" I was sure I'd heard incorrectly.

"Never mind," he said, extending his hand. "Cy Dittmer."

"Pleased to meet you," I said. "Jake Randall."

"Nice to meet you, Jake," he said. "You look familiar. Have we met before?"

"Not that I know of," I answered. But at the same time I got an odd feeling. I didn't think I'd met him before, but he felt familiar. The *shop* felt familiar.

"Do you have the machine with you?" he asked.

I felt stupid. I should have gone back for it when I saw the name of the shop.

"No, I don't," I said. "I can run and get it. I didn't know you were open."

"Of course you didn't." he smiled. "How could you?"

"How fast can you fix it?" I asked. "I'm . . ."

"You're a writer, and in the middle of a story. I understand."

"You do?"

"Better than you know. I should be able to fix it almost immediately."

"I'll be back in five minutes."

"I'll be waiting," he said.

I didn't answer. I rushed out the door, Ethel's story pushing me.

* * *

I walked back in the house, and nearly ran to the typewriter. Heaved the case onto the desktop, opened the buckles, and slipped the machine inside. Secured the two levers that held the feet in place for transport.

The laptop of its era. The portable word processor.

My eye caught on the stack of paper, the page on top missing the 'd's. I grabbed a manila envelope, shoved the pages inside, and brought the manuscript with me.

It was all I could do not to take the typewriter from the case, roll in another sheet of paper, and start typing. Missing 'd's be damned. I'd write them in if I had to.

But the shop was five minutes away.

Mr. Dittmer said he could fix it immediately.

He appeared to already know what might be wrong with it.

I lifted it, the weight feeling good on my arm, and carried it to the passenger side of the Jeep. I placed it carefully on the seat.

Normally, I didn't go anywhere without my real laptop. It was almost a joke around town. But I didn't grab it this time. I hoped the typewriter would be fixed by the time I was done eating.

Ethel was calling me. So was Naomi, her odd neighbor.

And a little boy. I didn't know his name yet, but I knew I would tell his story, too.

Whatever it was.

* * *

The Ghost Hole is a bar and grill. It isn't the greatest place for fish and chips in Garibaldi, but they're good, especially paired with cold beer, and it was across the street from the new typewriter shop. I went there often, ordering and sitting in the corner to write.

"No laptop today, Jake?" the waitress asked. Gabrielle was her name.

"Not today. Getting my typewriter repaired." I nodded at the shop across the street.

"He just opened. I wonder how he plans to stay in business? There can't be that many typewriters in town."

"Well, I have one. I might keep him open a day or two."

"Hope he makes it," she shook her head. "Haven't met him yet."

"Nice fella. Kind of odd," I told her. "I'm sure he'll be around at some point."

"The usual?" she asked.

"Sure," I said.

I didn't look at her, though. I studied the shop across the street. The light from the windows was bright, and I could see to the back of the store.

When I'd handed over the typewriter, offering the same explanation as before, Cy Dittmer's eyes widened just slightly, though I didn't say anything new.

And he'd told me to return in half an hour.

Then he'd gone to the back of the shop and exited through a door. Oddly, I heard a lock turn.

I'd left by the front door, puzzled. The shop filled the square footage of the building, at least as far as I could remember. How could there be a room back there? There were no stairs to a second story either . . . there was no second story. And as far as I knew, there was no basement. Where did he go?

As I ate, I waited for him to reappear, keeping my eyes trained on the back door.

After almost exactly thirty minutes, when my beer was down to a quarter, and I had a bite of fish and three fries left in the basket in front of me, I saw movement in the store.

I shoved the last bite and the fries in my mouth at the same time, washed them down with the final swig of beer, and stood, dropping a twenty onto the table.

My brain itched again.

* * *

"All ready?" I asked.

"As good as new," he answered with a smile.

"Excellent," I said. "How much do I owe you?"

"Nothing, this time. Fixing it is my pleasure."

"Really? I should give you something for your trouble," I said.

"Just one favor?" he asked.

"Sure, if I can."

"Let me read your story when it's done."

"Of course," I said.

I got into the Jeep, and looked at the folder on the seat.

And the Ghost Hole across the street.

The typewriter was portable. I didn't need any power.

The restaurant was noisy enough no one would mind the clacking of the keys.

It was only five minutes to home. But only a few steps across the street.

The itch was maddening.

I grabbed the case, the folder, and walked over.

"Back again?" Gabrielle asked.

"Yeah, just a beer," I said.

I set the case and folder on the table, then smacked my forehead.

I had the story, and the typewriter, but no extra paper.

I opened the case anyway.

The smell overwhelmed me, overpowered the smell of beer and peanuts in the bar, the fish frying in the kitchen.

Ink. Paper. The rubber of the roller.

Intoxicating.

Itching.

On top of the typewriter sat about twenty sheets of paper.

A yellow post it note sat on top of the blank sheets.

"Happy writing," was written across it in a beautiful, steady cursive.

I took the typewriter from the case, and closed it. Set it on the floor. Centered the machine in front of me on the table.

Rolled in a fresh sheet of paper. And started to type.

* * *

"The murder?" Ethel asked.

"Yes," Naomi said. "A family lived here. Mother, father, daughter, and a boy."

"A boy?" Something nudged the back of Ethel's mind.

"Yes. There was something wrong with the boy."

"Did they live here long?"

"No. They moved here from some small town in Idaho."

I stopped typing. It couldn't be. It wasn't *his* story.

"Do you remember the name?" Ethel asked.

She asked for me. I needed to know.

"Something-Falls, I am pretty sure. Not Idaho Falls, but something like that."

"Okay . . ." Ethel was genuinely curious. "So what happened?"

Naomi sighed. As if she didn't really want to tell the story, but knew she must.

"Like you, when they moved here the lot was empty. The house on the lot before was demolished. It had a bad foundation, and the walls were cracking.

"Doesn't take long after that. Around here that means your house is going 'south,' what they call it when a home slides down the side of the hill into the bay."

"I've heard of that," Ethel said. "My contractors were very insistent on reinforcing the existing foundation."

"Smart men. Do you know why folks thought it was so odd when you showed them your plans for the house you wanted to build?"

"Not really."

"The house the family built burned to the ground. That's the way I . . . we thought the family died. Then some special investigators came in, called in by the family or someone, we thought."

"What did they find?"

"They were all murdered. Except for the boy, of course."

"The boy?"

"Yes, the boy."

"He survived?"

"He did it, Ethel. He killed his family, or at least that's what the paper said."

"What does that have to do with my house?" Ethel gestured around.

"Your house looks exactly like theirs."

"Exactly? Impossible. I came up with the idea myself. Sketched it out sitting right there in the driveway, looking at the property."

"And the decorations?"

"Same thing. I just thought of what would look good in here."

"They're identical, Ethel. Identical."

"How do you know, Naomi?"

"Because I was the last one to see the family alive. I had a cup of coffee, right here, with Mrs. Fredrickson, the morning of the fire."

"How awful!"

"She wasn't herself, Ethel. She knew something bad was going to happen."

"What happened to the boy?"

"He went away, to prison, or juvie, or an institution, we all assumed," Naomi said.

Gabrielle tapped me on the shoulder.

"Hey, we're closing soon," she said.

I looked around. The place was empty. Everyone had gone home. The speakers were silent, and the clatter of dishes being washed behind the bar was the only sound.

"Five minutes?" I asked.

"Sure," she said. She cleared my beer glass, still half full, and didn't offer me another. I didn't ask for one either.

"That's horrible, Naomi," Ethel said.

"It is. The whole family was...they said he stabbed them all over and over."

"How did the fire start?"

"He started it in the kitchen. They had a hollow rooster, a toothpick holder, but filled with matches standing in it, tips up. She used them to light the stove."

Ethel looked over to the window sill, where Naomi's gaze settled.

A rooster just like she'd described stood there.

The rooster was filled with matches, tips up.

Ethel had found it in a second hand shop in town. Thought it was cute, and the matches were a perfect touch.

And practical. She could use them to light the old stove she'd picked up.

A gas model, made before they had automatic igniters. It had one installed, but she still liked to light it the old fashioned way.

She looked over at the old range, then at Naomi.

Who nodded, her eyes red, as if she might cry at any moment.

"He opened the gas lines. Set the rooster in the middle of the table, and lit one match in the center. At least that's what the fire inspector said."

"How did they know?"

Naomi shook her head.

"I have no idea. But the rooster, I found it in the yard."

"What did you do with it?" Ethel asked, suddenly afraid to know.

"I smashed it, on the corner of the foundation. Threw it down as hard as I could, and then kicked the pieces into the center of the ashes."

"But I bought this—"

"I know," Naomi said. "And the paintings, and the rest. Online. In town. All over the place. And yet . . ." Naomi trailed off.

"You're sure it's all exactly the same?" Ethel asked.

"Exactly."

Ethel shivered, and stared around her. The women were silent for a few moments.

"I need to head home," Naomi said. "Sorry to freak you out, Ethel, but I had to tell you."

"No, thank you," Ethel told her. "I'm glad you did."

Naomi left, and Ethel looked around the room.

She should have felt the presence of the ghosts before, but somehow she missed it.

"Are you here?" she asked the empty room.

The rooster rattled on the window sill.

A single match separated from the others, rose above them.

It did not move, but there was a sound of striking.

It lit, and Ethel watched breathlessly as it burned toward the others.

Just before the flame reached them, a breeze blew through the kitchen, and it went out. All the windows and doors were closed.

Shaking, she asked the room, "Who's there?"

But her senses told her whatever presence had been there was gone now.

She headed to bed, thinking there was no way she'd sleep.

But as soon as her head struck the pillow, she did.

And dreamed of mountains surrounding a large lake. An eerie church steeple peeked out of the water, as if the church itself were under the waves.

Ethel felt like she'd never been there before. And yet, the whole scene seemed familiar.

"You really have to go now, Jake" Gabrielle said.

Normally they were quite patient with me. The local writer was expected to be odd, and do strange things.

But clearly I'd overstayed my welcome this time.

"Sorry," I said, slipping the new pages into the folder, and packing away the typewriter.

I looked across the street.

The typewriter repair shop was dark, closed for the night.

* * *

The sun came through the window, and found my hand hovering over the green keys, a steaming cup of coffee beside me.

I remembered getting up. I remembered starting the coffee maker.

But I didn't remember getting out the typewriter.

I didn't remember pouring the coffee.

And I looked down on top of the folder and saw there were two freshly typed pages.

I didn't remember writing them.

Rolled into the typewriter was a third page.

Outside, the mists of Garibaldi seemed to have blended with the mists of Ridge Falls and filled my head.

I couldn't see through the fog.

Shaking my head, I picked up the two pages, and read.

Ethel woke with a start, looking at the clock.

7:30. She never slept that late.

But her dreams the night before had been odd, compelling. She felt what she imagined being hung over would feel like. She'd never been drunk, and never tried drugs. Sure, there was the one time after too much champagne on New Year's Eve when she'd awakened with a slight headache . . . but a mimosa cured it, and she hated the feeling so much, she always watched her drink intake after that.

Her mouth tasted like cotton, and she was sure her breath smelled worse.

So she headed straight to the bathroom, brushed her teeth and hopped in the shower. While she was rinsing, she swore she heard a knock at the front door. Ethel wasn't expecting anyone. If it was important, they would come back.

The knock came a second time, and she shut off the water, irritated.

Ethel grabbed her robe, and headed for the door, but as she did, a motor started up. A brown truck drove up and out of the driveway as she watched.

Odd, she wasn't expecting any deliveries.

Curious, she opened the front door to see if he'd left a note. And came face to face with Naomi, about to knock.

"Hi, Ethel," she said.

"Hi, Naomi, what brings you over this . . ." But she trailed off. Her neighbor held a package under her arm.

It was thin, like a book.

"The driver came over and got me. Said you weren't answering. This came signature required, priority."

"I wasn't expecting anything."

"Well, here it is either way." Naomi handed the package over.

Ethel took it, but her neighbor just stood on the porch, watching.

"Thank you?" Ethel said, adding the question mark.

"Aren't you going to open it?"

Ethel looked at the package in her hands. Too thin to be a book, she realized, almost the size of an 8 by 10 picture frame, but slightly larger.

Turned it around to read the label. The return address was a UPS store. In Pocatello, Idaho.

She didn't know anyone in Pocatello.

"Come on in," she said. "Let me get a knife and get this open." Naomi followed her to the kitchen.

The living room felt cold, colder than the morning outside.

Ethel slid a knife from the block, a Cutco, but new. An old one she'd found online. One that looked perfect in this kitchen.

She slid it under the tape and opened the box.

Yes, a framed picture. In it, a father stood with a hand on the shoulder of two children, one girl, one boy.

They stood next to a sign.

It was made of old wood, and the letters on it said simply:

"Welcome to Ridge Falls

Pop. 5739

Est. 1894

Moved 1944"

The boy was staring at her, into her eyes.

Naomi scr am d, and th l r ach d for h r should r.

I looked at the last line. It was supposed to say, "Naomi screamed, and Ethel reached for her shoulder."

But the 'e's were missing. The goddamn 'e's.

Only the most common letter in the English language.

I had to have it repaired again. Not later, now.

I hoped the shop was open. I hadn't seen a sign for the hours, and the owner had been open late the night before.

On the new sheet of paper, I tried to type a row of 'e's.

Nothing.

Not even the ghost of an impression.

Damn.

I turned the typewriter toward myself, and slowly pressed the key.

The striker rose toward me. Looked normal, just like the 'd' had.

Not a thing wrong with it, as far as I could tell.

"Screw it," I muttered, angry.

I threw the machine in its case, secured it, and hurried out to the jeep.

My stomach growled.

The only thing I'd had that morning was the coffee. As far as I could remember.

Maybe I could walk down to the diner, and grab some breakfast.

Then I looked at my watch.

11:00.

I'd totally lost track of time. No wonder I was hungry.

More like brunch then.

PART THR : TH 'E' FIX D

"Can you check the other keys?" I asked Cy.

"Check the other keys?"

"It's just I'm really into this story, and I hate to have to keep coming back."

"Sure, I can check them. But I don't think it will do any good."

Mr. Dittmer's mood seemed surly this morning, almost hostile. None of the chipperness from last time, though even then I thought it had been false, customer chatter.

"Thanks, I'd appreciate it if you could try anyway."

"Certainly, certainly." He smiled, but the expression never passed his lips, not even to touch his cheeks. His eyes remained cold.

"I'll be back. I'll just go grab some br—er, lunch."

"No problem," Mr. Dittmer said. He headed again for the door at the back of the store.

I walked outside. The morning mists had cleared, and the

day was gorgeous and warm. The wind would come later, as it always did in the afternoon.

I walked around the building. There were no additions on the back, and though there was a back door, large weeds growing from a crack in the sidewalk blocked it. It didn't appear the door had been opened in some time.

It just must be me, I thought. *There must be a small back room.*

But it didn't make any sense. It didn't seem to fit.

I left the Jeep parked, and walked two blocks down, toward the pier.

There was nothing wrong with fish and chips for brunch in Garibaldi. Nothing at all.

* * *

A half hour later, I collected the typewriter and headed home. I needed to know what Ridge Falls had to do with my story.

And I needed Ethel to take the photo out of the frame. Turn it over.

See the names there, and the dates, or the ages of the children.

Something.

There was something about that boy.

The way he looked at Ethel. At me, in my imagination.

Almost as if I knew him.

* * *

Naomi screamed, and Ethel reached for her shoulder.

"What's wrong?" she asked.

"It's them!"

"Who? The family who lived here?"

"Yes!"

"Who would send me this?"

"I don't know."

Ethel looked at the label again. A simple return address, and at the top, not a name, but a business.

UPS Store.

And the company logo.

A simple address.

And a phone number.

"Naomi, is this where they moved from?" she pointed to the sign.

"I think so."

Ethel went into the next room, and grabbed an old atlas. Turned to go back into the kitchen.

She had a computer, a laptop. (Didn't everyone?) But there was something about pages, about paper, when it came to maps, which computers couldn't match.

Naomi was right behind her.

Ethel sat down on the couch, and her neighbor joined her. She opened to the middle of the book.

I for Idaho.

Right before Iowa.

Opened the pages and ran her finger over the index in the right margin.

The one that listed the cities in alphabetical order.

Ridge Falls.

F-9

Near the bottom of the page. Just to the right of center.

There it was. The dot and the letters for it were tiny.

Grabbing a magnifying glass she looked closer.

It seemed to be next to a body of water.

Ethel wanted to know more.

She stood, and Naomi grabbed her hand.

"Where are you going?"

"To get my laptop. It's time for Google."

"Why Ethel?"

"Why what?"

"Why do you want to know more about where they are from?"

"Someone sent me this picture. I want to know who, and why."

"Why don't you call the UPS store?"

Ethel smacked her forehead. That would be a logical step.

She had a cell phone, but it was probably dead on her nightstand. She only charged and used it when it was absolutely necessary. She hated them.

She also had a land line, and the man who installed it bragged her package included unlimited long distance.

She never used that, either. Ethel had few people left in her family to call. The ones who were around communicated via social media or e-mail. The phone was almost an outdated form of communication and she often forgot she had it.

Ethel picked up the cordless handset, and punched the numbers on the return label of the package.

A singsong tone answered, followed by a mechanical voice.

"The number you have reached has been disconnected or is no longer in service. If you feel you have reached this recording in error, please check the number and try again."

Ethel did just that, sure she'd dialed correctly. The same message repeated.

"Damn!" she said, stabbing the button.

Naomi looked at her, and put her hand over her mouth.

"What did I do now?" Ethel asked.

"Just now, you sounded like . . . her."

"Like who?"

"Mrs. Fredrickson."

"The woman who lived here?"

"Yes."

"That's ridiculous."

"Ethel, I'm going home. You should come with me."

"I want to Google this town."

"You can do that from my house."

"No, Naomi. You're making me nervous."

"I intend to. You shouldn't be in this house."

"What do you mean? It's mine."

"I know. You built it. You decorated it. But it looks just like . . . before."

"Before?"

Naomi ignored the question mark in her voice, and went on.

"The outside. The color. The bushes near the house. The ones that burned in the fire."

"It's just coincidence."

"The inside, too? Ethel, there is something wrong here."

"It's just a package someone sent me. It doesn't mean a thing."

"It does, Ethel. You need to come with me."

"No."

"I'm leaving. If I leave, and you don't come, I'm not coming back."

"Maybe that is for the best." Her neighbor was going insane.

She shivered. It was cold in here today, and she could hear the heat running, seemingly without effect.

"I promise, if something strange happens, I'll come over. I'll leave."

"That's what she said. The day before she died. Before they all died."

"Naomi—"

"If you invite me to breakfast tomorrow, I'm not coming."

"If you don't want to come, that's fine."

"No, you'll invite me. And insist it's okay that I have already eaten."

"What are you talking about?"

"It's what's going to happen."

"I have no plans for that."

"Neither did she."

"What do you mean?"

"Déjà vu, Ethel. Déjà vu. It's going to happen, just like before."

"I won't. I promise. Nothing like that will happen."

"The picture. The boy is back."

"He's not."

"He is."

"Naomi, please."

"I'm going Ethel. Come with me."

"And then what?"

Naomi looked right and left, her face pale, her eyes darting in their sockets from object to object.

"Redecorate. Relandscape. Change things. All the things."

"Don't be ridiculous."

"Change all the things. Then he will stay away."

"You said the boy lived, Naomi. But you're talking like he's here, somehow influencing me."

"He did live. At first."

"What do you mean?"

"Just come Ethel."

"No."

"Then goodbye."

With that Naomi slipped out the door, and slammed it shut behind her.

Ethel watched out the living room window as the other woman fled across the lawn. About halfway across the shared driveway, she stopped and looked back.

Ethel was certain Naomi did not see her. Her neighbor crossed herself. Held up the sign of the evil eye. Kicked the dust off her shoes, and spun on her heel, practically running to her house.

Ethel shook her head. M ybe something w s going on, but she would sense it if it w s.

Wouldn't she?

She turned to go to her bedroom.

Get her l ptop. It w s time to do some rese rch.

* * *

The odd sound of the clacking keys woke me from my stupor.

I'd been in the zone, deep in the zone. Living with Ethel, following her around.

The bitch hadn't taken the picture from the frame yet. Hadn't turned it around. Seen the names and ages written there.

Sure, she was going to do some research on line. It seemed to be everyone's solution. But she needed to look at that picture. I needed to see it.

So did my readers.

s she he ded down the h llw y, Ethel dropped the fr me she didn't remember she'd been holding, nd the gl ss in the front

sh ttered on the floor. Ethel bent to pick it up, nd turned the photo over. Written on the b ck were the words

I looked at the last paragraph. The last line. Before that.

Fuck.

Fuckin' 'a' to be exact.

Not as popular as 'e' but still a pain in the ass.

I could keep going. Write them in, if I needed to. Sure, that would work, at least for a bit.

I grabbed a pen.

Rolled the sheet up.

Filled in the 'a's from the last few lines.

Sure. Looked good.

Put my fingers on home row. And nothing came.

I had no idea what the words were, what to type next.

Goddamn it.

Another trip to the typewriter shop.

I put the machine in its case, in what was becoming a familiar ritual, added some extra paper and the pages I had just typed to the folder. Carried it out to the Jeep, and headed out for the short drive to town.

I looked at the clock. 4:00 p.m.? Where had the day gone? My stomach growled. Eating out and visiting the typewriter repair shop was becoming habitual.

PART FOUR: FUCKING 'A'

Five minutes to get downtown. That's all it took.

4:05 p.m.

In the window of a shop that had been open until late the evening before was something I had never seen.

Although the lights were blazing.

The dark curtains wide open.

The owner was nowhere in sight.

And the sign read, "Sorry, We're Closed."

Unexpected. I got out and went to the door. Peered around the room.

Typewriters lined several shelves. Many had price tags on them, but several had folded card stock over the keys that said, "Customer Unit. Not for sale."

Customer Unit?

How many customers could he have in Garibaldi? Even the surrounding area? Hardly anyone had typewriters anymore, and if they did, they were for decoration. Not practical use.

I cupped my hands, struggled to see more. Behind the central counter were a few boxes. One said "Parts, Misc." The other said: "Ribbons."

Other shelves were still empty. The rest of the parts must be in the back room.

The back room. I willed movement there, for the door to open. But it remained closed.

Ethel's story buzzed in the back of my head, an itch that couldn't be scratched other than by writing. And the only way I could write it was on this damn machine. With letters that stopped working for no apparent reason.

If I hadn't found a repair shop so close, I'd have given up already. If I could. But that's the other thing. When a story grabs you as a writer, it's like a rhythm you can't resist. It comes on the radio and you have to dance. Have to sing along.

Have to.

I decided to look around back. It seemed like the proprietor, Cy Dittmer, lived here. I'd never seen a car, a bicycle, though that wasn't unusual in Garibaldi. But I'd never seen him leave, either. Just the store lights go dark.

There was that back door, though. Last time I'd seen it, it looked unused. I had to look again.

Had no choice.

Maybe Cy was back there, smoking. Hadn't his fingers been stained yellow, like those of a heavy smoker? Had there been the stale smell of cigarette smoke hanging around him?

Probably wishful thinking.

It wasn't yet dark. In fact, the sun stayed in the sky quite late this time of year, although the days were getting shorter. The afternoon breeze brought the smell of the town and the surrounding hills down to Main Street. People were cooking dinner, many grilling outside. The mixed smell of food and charcoal made my stomach growl loudly.

Coming around the back wall, I saw the door. It still looked unused, was still closed. There was no Mr. Dittmer puffing away on a Marlboro. Moving closer, I saw the ground around the door was filled with gravel. There didn't appear to be any footprints, and there were no cigarette butts scattered around. In fact, it didn't seem like anyone had used the door in years.

There were no windows on the side of the building, but my grandfather was a carpenter, and I was pretty good at estimating size and distances. If my eye was correct, there was no space for a back room of any size in the rear of the shop. Yet the owner seemed to disappear back there frequently, to work, to retrieve parts. I'd have to look again next time I was inside.

As I walked the side of the building, I counted my paces. Twenty-seven.

It would be easy enough to estimate the inside length of the building that way. In case my eyes were deceiving me.

As I rounded the corner, I saw the shop was now dark. The lights out.

Shit.

I'd have to wait until morning, and I didn't think I would be able to do that. I needed to write. I needed supper first, though, so decided to go to Pirate's Cove. The shrimp were simply to die for, and it should not be busy tonight.

I got in the Jeep and started the motor, glancing back at the shop.

Something moved in the darkness. I could have sworn it.

Annoyed, I drove away.

* * *

The meal was great, as always. Whether it was the local shrimp, the Tillamook salted butter, or a combination of the two, the large prawns tasted like lobster. A small slice of heaven.

By the time I got home, I should have been tired. A large beer, a large meal. Hell, I'd even splurged on dessert.

Despite the frustration caused by the typewriter, the writing had been going so well.

I thought I would drop into bed, exhausted and happy.

But I carried in the machine, and set it in its usual spot, still in the case. It called to me. Or, rather, the story did.

Opening the case I looked at the last page I'd typed.

shattered on the floor. Ethel bent to pick it up, and turned the photo over. Written on the back were the words

That last line. The itch.

It was only the 'a's. At least I'd gotten past the 'e' breaking. Even the 'd'. How common could 'a's be?

I'd write for a short while. I could fill them in by hand. It couldn't be that hard, could it?

* * *

photo over. Written on the back were the words:

Fredrickson Family. Dean, Samantha, Dean Jr., Shannon.

Something fluttered to the floor. A newspaper clipping.

From the Headlight-Herald.

"Family Dies in Fire. Son Held for Questioning"

by Sherry Briscoe.

The Fredrickson home in Bay City caught fire last night. Neighbors called 9-1-1, and thanks to rapid response to by the Garibaldi Rural Fire District, the blaze did not spread to the gardens surrounding the home, or to any other structures. However, tragically, the mother, father, and one of the children were trapped inside, and perished in the blaze.

The Tillamook County Sheriff also responded, and took the only survivor, Dean Fredrickson Jr., into custody.

"The fire does not appear to have been an accident," a spokesman for the Sheriff's Department said. "An investigation is underway, and we've called in a specialist to examine the scene. We expect autopsies to be complete by the end of the week."

When asked how the fire was determined to be not accidental so quickly, and why the young survivor was being detained, the spokesman had no comment.

Nor would he comment on what, exactly, the juvenile was being charged with.

Ethel went to her desk. Sat down in front of her laptop, and looked around the room.

The curtains, with pink roses and green vines twisting through sheer fabric looked old fashioned. Something not normally her taste.

But she'd seen them in the store, and they felt so right for this room. So right, and she had no idea why.

The carpet, a bland gray. Cheaper than she usually liked. Ethel was a woman of means, she could have afforded better. In fact, that was the case with many of the decorations in the house, she realized.

Looking around, the room suddenly felt cheap. Much of the furniture she'd purchased used.

Ethel did not normally buy used furniture.

She bought new. Elaborate. If she wanted something she could not find, she had it made.

Maybe Naomi was right. Maybe she should get out.

The room felt cold. So cold.

Whose room had this been? The boy's?

No, the girl's. She felt it now. She'd put a bed in here, in case of guests. But only a twin, and with old style headboards. Almost like the ones she and her sister had on their bunk beds.

Almost like . . .

She looked closer.

Then left the room. Ran to the other guest room, where she'd put another twin bed. Foolish, she realized now, but she'd not considered the small bed in regards to adult-sized visitors. While it was unlikely she would have guests in the first place, if she did, they'd probably be couples, and want to share a bed. A twin was a truly poor choice.

The headboard and footboard on the boy's bed looked almost identical to the girl's. The boy. Dean Jr.

The girl. Shannon.

Ethel rushed to her laptop.

It's not possible, she thought. I bought them in entirely separate places.

She opened her browser. Hit search.

Typed in Dean Fredrickson, Jr., and hit enter.

An article came up, first in the list, from the Ridge Falls Gazette.

"Boy's Body Found in Reservoir Identified"

A body found in the Ridge Falls reservoir last week by a fisherman has been identified as Dean Fredrickson, Jr., 19. Dean moved away with his family several years ago, and no one knew he was back in the area.

The Fredrickson family were longtime residents of Ridge Falls. David Fredrickson, now deceased, worked on the original dam project. His son, Dean, with his wife, Samantha, moved to Oregon, and the family passed away in a mysterious fire. The youngest boy, Dean Jr., 13 at the time, survived, and at first was charged with arson and possible homicide.

An investigation cleared him, but the boy disappeared from the foster home where he awaited adoption five years ago, and has not been seen since.

The police are attempting to determine if there are any surviving relatives, but so far have had no luck.

If you are related to this family, or are aware of anyone related to them, please contact the Ridge Falls Sheriff's Department.

That was all. The next entry was for an older man, a profile on a professional social media site.

So Dean Jr. was dead. The whole family was gone.

But something, someone had driven her to decorate like this. Suddenly it didn't feel like her house at all.

Ethel wanted to do what Naomi said, wanted to leave. Go over there. Come back tomorrow, and redecorate. She went to the kitchen, grabbed a glass of water, and drank it all.

Went to her bedroom to grab a few things. Pack. Just go.

But when she got there, felt suddenly very tired.

I'll just lay dow for a seco d, she thought to herself.

As her head hit the pillow, she fell i to dark ess, a d a deep sleep.

The ext thi g she k ew, the su was shi i g i the wi dow. It was mor i g.

I looked at the last line. Shit. Now the 'n' wasn't working either.

First the 'd'. Then the 'e'. Then the 'a'. And now, the 'n'.

D-E-A-N.

Not possible.

I had to stop writing. But I couldn't. I needed to know what happened. To Ethel. To Naomi. But I'd be damned if I was going to fill in all the 'a's and the 'n's. Especially with the name Naomi.

I had a feeling she would be coming back into the story, and I sure wasn't going to fill in the first two letters of her name every time she did.

Scanning what I'd written, I filled in the 'a's. It took

longer than I thought. Of course, I had written more than I planned.

When I was done, I filled in the 'n's on the last couple lines.

I'll just lay down for a second, she thought to herself.

As her head hit the pillow, she fell into darkness, and a deep sleep.

The next thing she knew, the sun was shining in the window. It was morning.

Put the typewriter into its case.

Shook the cramp out of my hand.

Then looked at the clock.

2 a.m.

No chance the repair shop would be open now.

I'd just have to sleep on it, if I could.

I went to my bedroom, lay down on top of the covers, and shut my eyes, praying for sleep.

* * *

Sunlight stabbed into my eyelids. I tried to get up, realized my legs were stuck in place. I'd been sitting too much. In front of the goddamn typewriter. If I could just finish this story. If I could just get Ethel to 'The End.'

Wherever that was.

I didn't seem to be able to work on anything else, and the typewriter was the only way I seemed able to tell Ethel's story. Stretching the best I could in the bed, I tried to work the kinks out. Reached over my head, and straightened my body to its full length. Pointed my toes. Flexed my fingers, my hands, and my wrists. Using a typewriter was hard, especially when you were used to a light touch, ergonomic keyboard. No wonder those old time secretaries never got carpal tunnel. Their forearms were tough, their fingers muscular.

Right then I determined to continue to type on a typewriter, even when this story was done. *At least my hands would stay in shape*, I thought, looking down at my gut, grown more ample over the last year. I needed to walk more, start running again maybe.

Hell, my shoulders were stiff, not just from sitting and typing, but from hauling the big case and heavy typewriter back and forth to the repair shop. And sitting in awkward places to type.

But damn if the story didn't call me right now. I needed to get words down, and to do that I needed to get into town, get to the shop, and get the typewriter fixed.

Or reset. Or whatever Cy Dittmer was doing to it.

His shop seemed busy with other machines, but if he never charged me, how could he possibly be making a living?

Truth be told, I didn't care. Making my way out to the kitchen, I looked around. It was a mess. I hadn't straightened it in days. A bag of coffee was open on the counter, the scoop sitting next to it with some grounds scattered around. I sniffed it. Not as strong as I usually liked. I almost always closed the bag and put it in the freezer to keep it fresh.

When was the last time I'd made coffee?

There were a few drops of liquid left in the bottom of the carafe, so maybe the night before?

One of the three or four mugs I used sat next to the case on the table. There was a ring around it. At least I didn't take cream, so there was no curdling crud stuck to the bottom. I picked it up and carried the mug toward the kitchen, suddenly remembering my ex-wife.

She'd left Ridge Falls before I did, looking vulnerable and frightened when I told her I wasn't going with her.

"Then you're going to die here," she'd told me. "But I won't. And I won't watch it happen to you."

The last straw for her simply came before it did for me. For her, it was the night the cat's body was found in our neighbor's yard. The vet found no blood left in the corpse, no marks on the body.

"I'm staying," I told her. But I'd left six months later. After the body of the boy was found the exact same way. On the shore of the reservoir this time.

She'd been the one who loved her creamer, and flavored syrups, and lattes. I'm the plain, black coffee type.

One pot a day. I used to drink more. In another lifetime. Before Ridge Falls. Before Garibaldi. Before Ethel, and Naomi, and Dean Sr., and Dean Jr., and a dead family.

They are characters in a story.

"Do you really believe that?" I asked myself out loud. The laugh that followed sounded wrong. Insane. More like a cackle.

Looking at the typewriter the whole time, I dumped a couple of scoops of coffee into the basket. Filled the back of the coffee maker with water. Turned it on. Leaned down, taking my eyes from the case for a moment, and grabbed a pan.

My stomach growled. It felt like all I'd been doing was typing the last few days. Interrupted by a little sleep. When had I last eaten? Everything was such a blur. I caught sight of the clock.

9:00 a.m.

The light in the fridge revealed almost nothing. A splash of milk in the bottom of a half gallon, one lonely egg in the holder on the door. I'd have to grab breakfast somewhere. And then a few groceries. *Why break precedent, right?* I could do those things while Mr. Dittmer fixed my typewriter.

Then I could spend the rest of the day writing.

Maybe into the night.

Maybe, just maybe, I could finish this story.

After all, the keys should all keep working now.

They'd passed along their message.

D-E-A-N.

Even if I had no idea what it meant.

* * *

The sign said Open, so I rushed through the door.

No one was there.

The space behind the counter was empty, and a quick survey of the shop revealed it to be the same.

No Cy. No customers.

I remembered my pacing from outside the day before.

Was that only yesterday? It must have been.

Last night.

How many was it? Twenty-seven?

Sounded about right.

After setting the case on the counter, I walked back to the front door. Picked the straightest line I could toward the back wall. One, two, three.

Counting my steps, but looking up to stay on target, I reached the back wall.

Twenty-six.

Assuming my paces were about three feet, a fair guess, which left . . .

No room for a back repair area at all. In fact, that could be counted as just a difference in the length of my stride.

Or the width of the old walls.

But it certainly wasn't enough difference for a room.

I looked at the door. There was a keyhole on this side of the knob, which meant it could be locked. But might not be.

Glancing left and right, making sure no one had come in behind me, I reached for the knob.

Then stopped.

I'd never seen anyone else in the shop, besides myself and the proprietor. Not a single customer.

I certainly hadn't been here the entire time he was open, at least that I knew of.

But the room was full of typewriters.

Where did they come from?

From wherever that room leads, I told myself.

Suddenly I was very cold. Like Ethel in the story. When she realized the house was full of . . . full of what?

Ghosts? Did I think Cy Dittmer was a ghost? That the typewriters, the whole shop, was an illusion?

I went to one of the typewriters first. An old Underwood. The keys were pristine. I couldn't imagine what could be wrong with it.

Reaching out, I felt the ridges of the letters on them, pushed one down gently, and watched the striker rise toward the empty carriage.

"Can I help you, Mr. Randall?"

I jumped. "Sorry," I said. "I was just looking around while I waited."

"Please don't touch the other machines—"

"Sorry," I said again. "I just—who does this one belong to?"

"An out of town customer. It's a beauty, isn't it?"

"Indeed," I said. "What's wrong with it?"

"It just needed some minor—adjustments."

Then I felt it. A breeze. It carried a smell, a damp odor I'd smelled before.

It smells just like Ridge Falls. That fucking reservoir.

Fucking fish, and fucking damp moss on the shore, just like the last time . . .

The last time I was in Ridge Falls. The last straw. The event that pushed me over the edge, to put the house on the market, and screw whether it sold or not. The night they found the boy.

I hadn't wanted to go look. But I hadn't been able to help myself. Usually I heard the reports the next day. Strange sightings, strange lights, something or someone dead or mysteriously missing.

Fucking Ridge Falls.

But that night, I'd heard it on the scanner, something I rarely left turned on. But that night had been an exception. I sat, reading a Stephen King novel, TV off. The scanner interrupted my thoughts at full volume.

"Holy Jesus, I need a bus now! At the south dock!" Retching sounds followed, by another curse. "Shit, hurry!"

The deputy, for that was who it turned out to be, eventually stopped keying his mic, and the sheriff broke in.

"We're on the way Gary. Stay the fuck off the radio, unless you want the whole town to show up."

But it was too late for that. People were curious, morbidly so. Even in Ridge Falls, where normal was simply not normal. Not to mention the Ridge Falls Gazette reporter, owner, and occasional substitute paper boy. Against my better judgment, I went.

Before they covered the body I saw the boy. Then the whispers came through the crowd.

"Not a mark on him."

"No blood left in the body though, so Richie said. Light as a feather."

I went home and packed. Headed here, to my retreat in Garibaldi, and just never went back.

I wonder if Dean Sr. had felt the same way. If he'd seen something, gotten spooked, and packed up the family in one night.

I could imagine the scene.

"Get in the car, kids."

"But Dad!"

"No buts. Grab all of your clothes. Whatever you can carry. We're moving."

"Dean, what are you thinking?" Mrs. Fredrickson would have said.

Dean had a sister. Sarah. Suddenly I knew it. Knew it as well as I knew home row. As well as I knew how to type.

As well as I could feel, when typing on the old Royal, when the paper was about to run out, and I was about to be screwed, and type right off the end, and I would grab, without thinking, another blank sheet, and roll it in.

Start the next line right where I left off.

"Never mind what I'm thinking," Dean Sr. would have told them, his nostrils full of that smell, the vision of the lights over the east end of the reservoir, reflecting in the water. Lights that could not, should not have been there.

Lights that appeared every so often, usually around the same time the water took someone else.

The monster in the water, Dean might have thought.

Thoughts so similar to mine.

Jesus H. Christ. I made Dean up, he isn't real. His boy hadn't grabbed a porcelain rooster filled with matches . . .

"Can I help you, Mr. Randall?"

I wasn't typing. I wasn't in Ridge Falls, or the story. Dean wasn't real, Sr. or Jr. They were both part of a story.

A story I made up.

But the smell, the breeze. Those were still there.

Over Cy's shoulder, I could see the door was open. The back door of the shop.

The one that couldn't lead anywhere, but did.

"Um, yeah," I said, trying to spit out the words.

Mr. Dittmer looked at my eyes. Looked where I was looking.

"My apologies," he said.

I wasn't sure if he was talking to me, or someone unseen in the mysterious back room.

He reached back and shut the door, and the spell broke.

"Yes," I said, clearing my throat. The world now seemed right. *Smelled* right.

"My typewriter. It's two letters this time. I'm not sure I understand it."

"Me either," he said. "Which ones?"

"The 'a' and the 'n'," I told him.

For a second, a tiny flicker of something showed in his face.

Was it fear?

It couldn't have been. Why would he be afraid?

"Odd," he said.

Just then my stomach growled again. Loudly.

"Why don't you go grab some breakfast? Give me about an hour this time."

"Sounds fine," I said, even though it didn't. I did need groceries, however. I did need breakfast.

But I had a greater need. Until the typewriter was fixed, I couldn't give in to that one.

My mind itched. God, it itched.

PART 5: THE END

"This isn't my typewriter," I said. It looked the same, it really did. Same metal gray body. Same green keys, in equally good shape.

But it wasn't mine. It looked at me, but it didn't say a word. From somewhere in the shop, mine was screaming at me. The screams were muffled, but I could hear them.

It had a story to tell. I was only the vehicle. To deceive myself and say I was anything more would have been dishonest. Not a stretch for a fiction writer, but a lie nonetheless.

Something in the story was real. Whether it was from another time, or an alternate universe, I had no idea.

But at least a part of the story was true. I was just telling it. Ethel was telling it to me, even as Naomi told some of it to her, and some she found out on her own.

But I needed to finish. There was an ending, happy or sad I did not yet know.

But Ethel's story needed to be told.

And because of Dean Sr., and his desire to move his family here, and because of me, who unwittingly followed in their footsteps, Ridge Falls and Garibaldi were forever connected.

"Sorry," the shop owner said, apparently seeing I'd spotted his error, or perhaps his deliberate substitution, right away. "I have two like this in the shop at the moment. I must have mixed up the invoices."

"Fine," I said, as he moved to get mine. I knew when he got to the case, without him telling me. "What's wrong with this one?" I asked about the one in front of me.

"Hmm?" he asked.

"What's wrong with this one?" I repeated. "Do the keys stop working on it, too?"

"No, no," he said. "Nothing that serious. Just needed a new ribbon. And the 'e' was hitting a little low."

"Ah," I said as he closed that case and offered mine in its place. I took it without opening it.

"You want to make sure that's the right one?" he asked.

"It is," I said with confidence, and walked out.

As I put it in the passenger seat of the Jeep, walked around to slide behind the wheel, I looked back at the shop.

From the door, Cy Dittmer watched my every move.

* * *

Naomi answered the phone.

"Can you come over for breakfast?" Ethel asked.

"No," Naomi said. "We already talked about this."

"I know. But I believe you now. Something—it just hit me last night. Come over, please?"

"I already ate."

"Just for a cup of coffee? I'm going to leave today, then hire

someone to come in. To redecorate, and re-landscape. Make this house my own."

"It won't work, Ethel. I'm not coming."

"I'm begging you, Naomi. Just this one time. Help me get the things that are mine out of here. I'm leaving, for sure."

"No."

"I need help. You're the only one I know who will help. Who knows why I have to do this."

"Ethel, I can't. If I do, the cycle will repeat itself."

"We won't let it. Don't you see?"

"I just can't."

"Please?" Ethel could feel the other woman's resistance over the phone, but her need for Naomi bordered on obsession. She'd woken up in a panic. Light streaming through the window.

This was the day.

She felt it. It was either leave, or redo what she had done.

Unwittingly done, she reminded herself. But still, she'd brought back an evil to this place, a fear back into Naomi's life. It wasn't right, it wasn't fair, and she needed to set things straight.

This was the only way she could think of.

But she couldn't do it alone.

From the receiver, she heard a deep sigh.

"Fine," Naomi said. "I'll be over. No coffee, no breakfast. We'll eat over here. We just grab your stuff and go."

"Yes, thank you," said Ethel. As she hung up, she turned around.

On the table were two plates, and two still steaming cups of coffee. When had she cooked breakfast? When had she put those there?

A knock came at the door, followed by it opening, and Naomi's voice.

"Hello?"

"In here," she called back, frozen to the spot.

Footsteps came, and then Naomi. As her friend entered the room, Ethel saw her put her hands to her face.

Cover her mouth.

"Ethel," she said. "I told you no."

"I didn't . . ." Ethel started. "I don't remember . . ."

"We have to go," Naomi said, grabbing her hand.

"My things," Ethel tried to resist. "My laptop. My—"

Naomi slapped her, hard. Ethel looked around the room.

Something smelled funny.

In the rooster, on the window sill, one match rose, separating itself from the others.

Ethel felt a steel grip around her arm. Pincers biting into her flesh, and pulling her along. Her feet hardly seemed to touch the floor and she moved them just to stay upright.

Someone was screaming in her ear.

Telling her, "Go! Go! Run!"

She wanted to. But, at the same time, wanted to stay.

Her son. Her daughter.

Shannon. Dean Jr.

She had to save them.

Samantha struggled to get free. Struggled to run back in. Something bad was about to happen.

Dean had done this. He brought them here. Brought them to this odd town on the sea to kill them.

She knew it.

Her husband was a bad man.

Then she saw him. Samantha saw him, pushing Shannon out the door. Calling to her.

"Get out! Get out!" he said. His arms waved frantically. Urging her onward.

"But Dean!" she cried out, meaning her son, not her husband.

"I'll get him," Dean Sr. said. "Just go."

Ethel turned, the claws still holding her arm, pulling her toward the front door.

And Dean Sr., Samantha's husband. Her husband. Her vision blurred as she became two women again.

Ethel looking back.

A mother looking back.

Seeing her only son, standing by the back door. Match in hand. Grinning.

Her head hit the doorframe. The ghost of the boy disappeared. So did the ghost of the man.

She smelled rotten eggs. Natural gas.

Ripped oxygen from the surrounding air, tried to fill her lungs through a raw throat.

She heard screaming, her own voice.

"My son! My son!"

Naomi answering. "He's not here Ethel. Come on!"

She stopped, let her voice go silent.

Her screaming ended, and she found her feet.

She'd seen them.

The ghosts. Maybe too late.

Found her legs, and straightened up, linking her arm in Naomi's, no longer fighting her.

Naomi knew what was coming.

So did Ethel, maybe better than her friend did.

So she ran, pushing her friend along.

Then a warm hand found her back. Pushed her forward and down toward the ground.

A second later a monster roared.

Rage. Heat.

Then there was no oxygen. Only hot water, and she was drowning in it.

Orange filled her vision, then red, then black. She closed her eyes.

Found her hands and knees. Crawled forward, Naomi by her side. She felt her more than saw her. It took an eternity.

It took ten seconds.

It took two minutes.

Then an eternity again.

The ball of fire expanded. Engulfed them. Retreated back into itself.

Oxygen made itself known. Not the clean, crisp kind that should have been in the sea air, but acrid and stale.

Still, it was breathable.

It was life.

Ethel sucked at it. Heard Naomi do the same.

A loud hiss, a wheeze, then an exhale.

Then another breath.

She heard herself gasp. Gasp again.

Looked down at the ground.

Her cell phone lay there, looking dead and useless.

But when she picked it up, the screen came to life.

"Emergency Call," it said under the lock screen.

Ethel raised a finger to touch that button.

The finger was black on the tip, red on the side. The nail was dirty. It belonged to someone else. Surely it did. That could not be her finger.

Her hand.

But she was grateful for its use, whoever it belonged to. Numbers came up. 9-1-1.

She hit send.

Heard nothing. The phone looked like it was working, but she put it to her ear.

Nothing.

Screamed into it. Or tried to.

"Help! Help! Send help!"

The words sounded faint, seemed to come from far away.

Ethel pulled the phone down. Looked at it. Red liquid dripped down the screen.

That made no sense unless…

Unless she was bleeding.

She dropped the phone into the grass. Put her hand to her ear. Felt wet, pulled it away, and looked at it.

Red. On the fingers not her own. But they were hers. She knew her own palm. Saw the lifeline. The one that seemed to stretch forever. Or so she'd been told by palm readers. Frauds, even though several had told her the same thing.

Ethel was sure she was dying.

Turning her head, she saw Naomi. Her neighbor sat, legs spread, ass on the grass.

Ass on the grass. That rhymes, Ethel thought to herself.

Naomi's top was torn. Rumpled. Her eyes were wide open, staring at something behind Ethel. Because she wasn't looking at her. Her mouth moved without sound.

It wasn't her Ethel had heard breathing earlier. It had been her own breathing.

For, as her grandmother would have said of her grandfather, at the moment Ethel was deaf as a post, only the pulse of her blood drumming in her head.

Naomi pointed, and Ethel turned to look.

The house was on fire. Not just on fire, engulfed. So was the garden. The landscaping. The amount and heat of the fire was impossible, and yet there.

In front of it, Ethel saw a figure. A young boy. A moment later he was joined by a man. A woman. A young girl.

Ethel could see the fire through them. They could not be real. They would cook that close to the flames.

She already felt her own face tightening over her bones, like when she'd gotten a severe burn in college from falling asleep on the beach, in the sun.

Spring break.

The California coast maybe. Maybe Mexico. Not Oregon.

Where she was now.

The boy faced his family.

The father, Dean Sr., she was sure, shook his finger at the boy.

The boy turned, gesturing to his mother. His sister.

They'd made it hard for the men, Ethel knew instinctively. Overbearing maybe. Bitches would be the word the boy used.

The boy had taken their abuse.

The father didn't. He struck back.

The boy held something in his hand. The porcelain rooster.

Dean Sr. reached for his son.

His son dropped the object and stepped free of the blaze.

And all of them disappeared.

As they did, the fire died down.

Ethel looked around her. The driveway, the space between her and Naomi's houses, pulsed with red and blue light.

The fire engines were right there. Cop cars parked crazily on the lawn behind them.

Still, the sirens wailed in what sounded to her like the distance. A great distance.

Another fire truck pulled up. Two hoses snaked toward her house, what was left of it.

Two more were turned on the lawn, flooding it.

A cop ran toward them. Knelt in front of her. He smelled like Axe. That cheap aftershave deodorant spray she saw on TV. He was young.

He mouthed words she could not hear clearly, yet understood.

"Are you okay?"

Ethel shook her head. She was most certainly not okay. Not at all, as a matter of fact.

He spoke into a mic clipped to his shoulder. He wore a sheriff's star.

He was much too young.

She saw his name tag.

Fredrickson.

Ethel screamed, and the officer grabbed her in a big embrace.

She heard the sound of her own voice in her head. Calling out for help.

Then he pulled back, but just a little.

"It's going to be okay," she read on his lips.

Then she felt the knife slip between her ribs.

She screamed again.

Then Naomi hit Dean, Jr. A flurry of support hose, diabetic shoes, and a flowered house dress, she tackled him with strength a linebacker would be proud of.

His face went from an evil grin to shock, to surprise, to rage.

Ethel tried to warn Naomi, tried to cry out.

But she didn't need to. Naomi knew the boy.

Naomi's feet lashed out in kicks, raining them on the deputy's body, head, thighs. He didn't have enough hands to protect everywhere.

A shoe hit him in the nuts.

Her side hurt, but Ethel managed to stand, then joined her friend, blood spurting through the blackened fingers pressed against her wound.

The deputy lay still. Curled into a ball.

Ethel stopped, breathing heavily. Suddenly the world swam, out of focus, and back in. She fell to a sitting position on the lawn. Bit her cheek as her butt hit the ground.

Moaned, tasted blood. Opened her mouth wide, and felt her ears pop. Sound rushed in.

Naomi sat next to her.

"Ethel?" Naomi said. "Are you okay?"

Ethel nodded, and then the tears came. She tilted toward her friend, and fell into her arms.

The last thing she remembered seeing was a group of men rushing toward them, some in brown sheriff uniforms, some in the blue of EMS. A few rushed to the fallen deputy.

Then the pain, the stress overtook her, and Ethel felt herself fall back onto the grass, eyes closed, her heart slowing...

I'll have to rebuild, she thought to herself dreamily.

But Ethel knew she would do no such thing.

* * *

I came out of the writing fog slowly. I didn't remember sitting down. Looked to my right, and saw an empty coffee cup, and empty glass, with some diminished ice cubes in the bottom, and an empty soda bottle next to that.

A large one.

Realized I needed to piss. Really bad.

Blinked, hardly able to see, to focus. Tried to stand.

At first my legs failed me. Pins and needles raced up and down them.

Then my body took over. The need to empty my bladder overriding the desire to wake my legs slowly.

I stood, staggered, and made my way down the hallway.

Got my pants undone just in time, and a second later heard the welcome, healthy stream splash into the water below.

No need to have my prostate checked. Things were flowing quite nicely, thank you.

Turned away and looked in the mirror.

My hair stood up, mussed as if I had run my fingers through it. I must have at some point.

Maybe several points.

Went to turn on the faucet, and noticed by hands. Swollen, red, cramped.

I wondered how much I'd written. The story felt nearly done. But only nearly so.

Then, in the distance, I heard sirens.

From the direction of main street.

The fire house.

Then the sound of police.

I needed to read the last part of what I'd written. I rushed back out to the living room.

On the couch was a pillow. And a blanket. Like someone had slept there.

I'd slept there. I knew it.

I took the few steps that brought me to the kitchen.

A loaf of bread lay open on the counter, the tie missing. The peanut butter was open next to it. A knife protruded from a jar of jelly, stuck up to the handle.

I opened the refrigerator. I knew I'd bought milk, eggs, a few other necessities.

Where were they?

9:45, the clock read.

It was 9:45 a.m.

Not p.m.

I'd worked all evening. All night, except for apparently some sleep on the couch.

I'd eaten. At least something.

Something I didn't remember fixing.

Jesus.

I walked over to the typewriter, and looked at the paper in the roller. The last line.

But Ethel knew, even then, she would do no such thing.

Flipped back a few pages, frantically looking for . . . something. Back to what I'd written before the typewriter broke the last time.

The next *thing she* knew, *the* sun *was shining* in *the window. It was morning.*

The next thing she knew, it was morning. The next thing I knew, it was morning.

Oh my god.

I ran outside.

The passenger door of the Jeep was open. I hadn't even shut it when I got home. In the back were the two grocery bags. I saw flashing lights racing down the shoreline road. The boxy shape of an ambulance was unmistakable.

In the distance, a column of black smoke rose into the sky.

I knew on the lawn of a shared driveway, the red and blue of sirens were painting the faces of two frightened ladies who'd narrowly escaped death.

I ran back to the Jeep, slamming the passenger door. Rushed inside and grabbed my keys. Left the typewriter. Left the manuscript.

The story . . . no. Not a story. The accounting.

Turned around in the driveway and swerved out onto the road, debating.

Left, toward Bay City.

Right, toward town.

Right. Five minutes later was on Main Street. Raced past the gas station, the grocery store.

Stopped in front of the Typewriter Repair Shop.

The windows were empty, dark and covered.

A sign hung on the door.

"For Rent."

I got out. Ran to the gas station.

Sam looked up as I rushed through the door.

"Hey, Mr. Randall," he asked. "What can I do you for?"

"The shop over there, Sam. When did the guy leave?"

"Shop next door? That place has been vacant for months."

"No. Remember. Last week, a guy rented it."

"He did. Came in, put up dark curtains, then cleared out. Never actually opened."

"What?"

"Heard he cancelled the lease."

"You're saying there wasn't a shop there?"

"A shop? No sir." Sam looked skeptical of my sanity. "Are you okay, Mr. Randall?"

"Not a typewriter repair shop?"

"Typewriter repair? Nowadays? Who'd need such a thing?"

"Who indeed?" I answered. "What are the sirens for?"

"Ethel Abrams place, up on the hill. Some kind of gas leak." He scratched his face, frowned. "Weirdest thing. The last place up there burned down too."

"So I heard," I said, and walked out.

I could feel Sam staring after me, but I didn't look back.

I strode to the back of the shop, that mysterious back door. Beside it was a fresh patch of mud, a boot track right in the center. I knelt down, took some of the dirt in my hand, and sniffed it.

Smelled just like Ridge Falls, and the reservoir.

I walked around the front of the shop. Still empty, although I looked in the window, hands cupped around my face.

Toward the back, I saw movement. Swore I did.

But I couldn't make it out.

Got in the Jeep and made a U-turn, driving toward Bay City.

* * *

I made a left, and headed up the hill. On the way, an ambulance passed me, clearly on its way down. No lights, no sirens. A good sign. Ethel was inside. Maybe Naomi too. But their injuries weren't serious. At least not life threatening.

A cop car passed me too. And one fire engine.

I got to the top, and found the driveway blocked. I went down a couple of driveways, turned around, and parked on the other side of the road.

As I got out and walked to the drive, I saw one cop car. Another ambulance, and one fire truck remained.

I tried to stroll casually down.

Thinking in the back of my head of something I had written, a few moments—hours?—before. I could see the page in my head.

The boy held something in his hand. The porcelain rooster.
Dean Sr. reached for his son.
His son dropped the object and stepped free of the blaze.

I could see the page, and at the same time see the spot from my imagination.

Naomi's house was exactly as I had pictured.

So was the drive, the lawn.

I knew without anyone telling me, the house had been the same. So was the fire.

I hadn't imagined it. I had seen it.

I walked through the scene, as if I knew what I was doing. A fire fighter glanced at me, continued hosing the house down. In the back of the ambulance, a woman sat. She looked at me, smiled, and waved.

I waved back at Naomi. Ethel must have been in the other one by herself.

To my left, a sheet covered a motionless form.

The sheet stirred as I walked by.

I ignored it.

A deputy appeared, an overweight older man. Carl, I thought his name was.

"Can I help you Mr. Randall?"

"Just need to look at something," I said.

"Afraid I can't let you . . ."

"Just one minute, Carl," I said, and walked past him. I don't know why he didn't stop me.

I approached the spot on the lawn where I'd seen the family standing. Where I'd seen the boy drop the object.

It was there. The porcelain rooster.

Picked it up. It was warm. A breeze whipped up. Leaves rustled.

Behind me, so did the sheet. That wasn't from the wind. I knew it.

But I'd fix that.

Cocked my arm back, and threw the rooster as hard as I could.

It landed in the middle of the smoldering embers that had been the house.

A brief puff of flame rose where it landed, and died with a hiss as the water from the hose hit it.

"You can't do that!" Carl said, but I turned around and brushed past him.

The sheet lay on the ground, to my right now, suddenly deflated.

There was nothing under it.

I kept walking, up the driveway toward my Jeep.

EPILOGUE

I like my new neighbors. A couple of ladies who used to live up on the hill bought the house next to me.

"We moved in together to share expenses," one told me when I went over to introduce myself. Her name is Ethel, she told me. Her friend is named Naomi.

They're kind. Even had me over for dinner. Some pretty good Italian food.

The gossip is they're lesbians. I think something deeper ties them together.

Their old houses shared a driveway up on the hill. Bay City, they said.

Ethel's burned. Kind of mysteriously.

So Naomi put her house on the market too. A younger couple from Idaho bought it, and the lot next door where Ethel's house once stood. They told the ladies they planned to plant some kind of garden there.

When they told me this, over dinner, it made me a bit uncomfortable. I really don't know why.

When I came home after dessert, I felt a story coming on.

Kind of like when you are getting that first fall cold. Even before the first symptoms hit, you just know it's unavoidable.

But instead of sitting down at my computer, like I usually do, I sat down at my old Royal typewriter. I'd just put in a new ribbon.

I liked to type on it sometimes. For old time's sake.

It's just like the one I learned to write on.

I rolled in a blank sheet of paper, and put my fingers on home row, wondering how the story might start.

Slowly, my fingers started to move, and words appeared on the page.

She never would have built the house there, if only she had known.

THE END

TLL 12-8-14

Did you enjoy this story? If so, I would love it if you could leave a review. It's something authors appreciate more than anything. I hope you are excited for the next chapter in Max's story.

Max's story is just beginning. And there are some other great stories coming soon. The next in the series, *Compelled*, will be coming this fall, and you won't want to miss it.

In a small town in Montana, a woman disappears, and her family suspects the worst.

And a serial killer, silent for three years, starts killing agin. .

Want to keep up with Max and his stories? Want free books and special offers, and starting soon, a free story every month? Subscribe to our newsletter on my website. We'll only send you bargain books and let you know when new stories are coming. You'll never miss a release.

Harvested is also available in audio format! Find it on Audible and other retailers where you listen to audiobooks.

If you want to join our exclusive review team, see our

website for more information. (There is a test, but it's an easy one, I promise!)

In the meantime, be well. More exciting fiction coming soon!

ABOUT THE AUTHOR

Troy Lambert is a full-time writer and author. Having written over two dozen mysteries and other novels, Troy is well-versed in story creation, and he knows what it takes to make a fictional story real! Troy's hobbies and pastimes (when he's able to break away from the computer) include hiking into the mountains of Southwest Idaho, fishing in a fast-rushing stream, and going for a drive where his mind can work on creating that perfect twist to the book he's currently writing. A native of Idaho Falls, Idaho, Troy and his wife live in Meridian, Idaho. You can find his other works, including his latest book, *Teaching Moments*, at troylamber-twrites.com.

ALSO BY TROY LAMBERT

THE MAX BOUCHER SERIES:

Teaching Moments

Harvested

THE SAMUEL ELIJAH JOHNSON SERIES

Redemption

Temptation

Confession

MONSTER MARSHALS

Miner Inconveniences

Tilting at Windmills

NON-FICTION

The Tao of Trek

Writing as a Business: Production, Distribution, and Marketing

7 Steps to Plotting Your Novel Quickly

THE DOG COMPLEX

Stray Ally

Book #15: "Offered in Oklahoma"*

*These books are now available in audio format!

All the books in the "Capital City Murders" series are available at www.CapitalCityMurders.com and your favorite e-book seller.

www.ingramcontent.com/pod-product-compliance
Lightning Source LLC
Chambersburg PA
CBHW031459130726
47989CB00003B/1465